PICTURE BOOK STUDIO

A Michael Neugebauer Book
Copyright © 1990 Neugebauer Press, Salzburg, Austria.
Published and distributed in USA by Picture Book Studio, Saxonville, MA.
Distributed in Canada by Vanwell Publishing, St. Catharines, Ont.
Published in UK by Picture Book Studio, Neugebauer Press Ltd., London.
Distributed in UK by Ragged Bears, Andover.
Distributed in Australia by Era Publications, Adelaide.
Printed in Italy.

Library of Congress Cataloging in Publication Data
Kipling, Rudyard, 1865-1936.
The sing-song of Old Man Kangaroo/by Rudyard Kipling;
illustrated by John Rowe.
Summary: Relates how the proud kangaroo became different from all
other animals.
ISBN 0-88708-152-5: $14.95
[1. Kangaroos—Fiction.] I.Rowe, John, ill. II. Title.
PZ7.K632Si 1990
[E]—de20   90-7382

RUDYARD KIPLING
JOHN ROWE

THE SING-SONC

OF OLD MAN KANGAROO

Not always was the Kangaroo as now we do behold him, but a Different Animal with four short legs. He was grey and he was woolly, and his pride was inordinate: he danced on an outcrop in the middle of Australia, and he went to the Little God Nqa.

He went to Nqa at six before breakfast, saying, "Make me different from all other animals by five this afternoon."
Up jumped Nqa from his seat on the sand-flat and shouted, "Go away!"
He was grey and he was woolly, and his pride was inordinate: he danced on a rock-ledge in the middle of Australia, and he went to the Middle God Nquing.

He went to Nquing at eight after breakfast, saying, "Make me different from all other animals; make me, also, wonderfully popular by five this afternoon." Up jumped Nquing from his burrow in the spinifex and shouted, "Go away!" He was grey and he was woolly, and his pride was inordinate: he danced on a sandbank in the middle of Australia, and he went to the Big God Nqong.

He went to Nqong at ten before dinner-time, saying, "Make me different from all other animals; make me popular and wonderfully run after by five this afternoon."

Up jumped Nqong from his bath in the salt-pan and shouted, "Yes, I will!"

Nqong called Dingo – Yellow-Dog Dingo – always hungry, dusty in the sunshine, and showed him Kangaroo. Nqong said, "Dingo! Wake up, Dingo! Do you see that gentleman dancing on an ashpit? He wants to be popular and very truly run after. Dingo, make him so!"

Up jumped Dingo – Yellow-Dog Dingo – and said, "What, *that* cat-rabbit?"

Off ran Dingo – Yellow-Dog Dingo – always hungry, grinning like a coal-scuttle, – ran after Kangaroo.

Off went the proud Kangaroo on his four little legs like a bunny.

This, O Beloved of mine, ends the first part of the tale!

He ran through the desert; he ran through the mountains; he ran through the salt-pans; he ran through the reed-beds; he ran through the blue gums; he ran through the spinifex; he ran till his front legs ached.

He had to!

Still ran Dingo – Yellow-Dog Dingo – always hungry, grinning like a rat-trap, never getting nearer, never getting farther, ran after Kangaroo.

He had to!

Still ran Kangaroo – Old Man Kangaroo. He ran through the ti-trees; he ran through the mulga; he ran through the long grass; he ran through the short grass; he ran through the Tropics of Capricorn and Cancer; he ran till his hind legs ached.

He had to!

Still ran Dingo – Yellow-Dog Dingo – hungrier and hungrier, grinning like a horse-collar, never getting nearer, never getting farther; and they came to the Wollgong River.

Now, there wasn't any bridge, and there wasn't any ferryboat, and Kangaroo didn't know how to get over; so he stood on his legs and hopped.

He had to!

He hopped through the Flinders; he hopped through the Cinders; he hopped through the deserts in the middle of Australia. He hopped like a Kangaroo. First he hopped one yard; then he hopped three yards; then he hopped five yards; his legs growing stronger; his legs growing longer. He hadn't any time for rest or refreshment, and he wanted them very much.

Still ran Dingo – Yellow-Dog Dingo – very much bewildered, very much hungry, and wondering what in the world or out of it made Old Man Kangaroo hop. For he hopped like a cricket; like a pea in a saucepan; or a new rubber ball on a nursery floor.

He had to!

He tucked up his front legs; he hopped on his hind legs; he stuck out his tail for a balance-weight behind him; and he hopped through the Darling Downs. He had to!

Still ran Dingo – Tired-Dog Dingo – hungrier and hungrier, very much bewildered, and wondering when in the world or out of it would Old Man Kangaroo stop.

Then came Nqong from his bath in the salt-pan, and said, "It's five o'clock." Down sat Dingo – Poor-Dog Dingo – always hungry, dusty in the sunshine; hung out his tongue and howled.

Down sat Kangaroo – Old Man Kangaroo – stuck out his tail like a milking-stool behind him, and said, "Thank goodness *that's* finished!"

Then said Nqong, who is always a gentleman, "Why aren't you grateful to Yellow-Dog Dingo? Why don't you thank him for all he has done for you?"

Then said Kangaroo – Tired Old Kangaroo – "He's chased me out of the homes of my childhood; he's chased me out of my regular meal-times; he's altered my shape so I'll never get it back; and he's played Old Scratch with my legs."

Then said Nqong, "Perhaps I'm mistaken, but didn't you ask me to make you different from all other animals, as well as to make you very truly sought after? And now it is five o'clock."

"Yes," said Kangaroo. "I wish that I hadn't. I thought you would do it by charms and incantations, but this is a practical joke."

"Joke!" said Nqong, from his bath in the blue gums. "Say that again and I'll whistle up Dingo and run your hind legs off."

"No," said Kangaroo. "I must apologise. Legs are legs, and you needn't alter 'em so far as I am concerned. I only meant to explain to Your Lordliness that I've had nothing to eat since morning, and I'm very empty indeed."

"Yes," said Dingo – Yellow-Dog Dingo – "I'm just in the same situation. I've made him different from all other animals; but what may I have for my tea?"

Then said Nqong from his bath in the salt-pan, "Come and ask me about it tomorrow, because I'm going to wash."

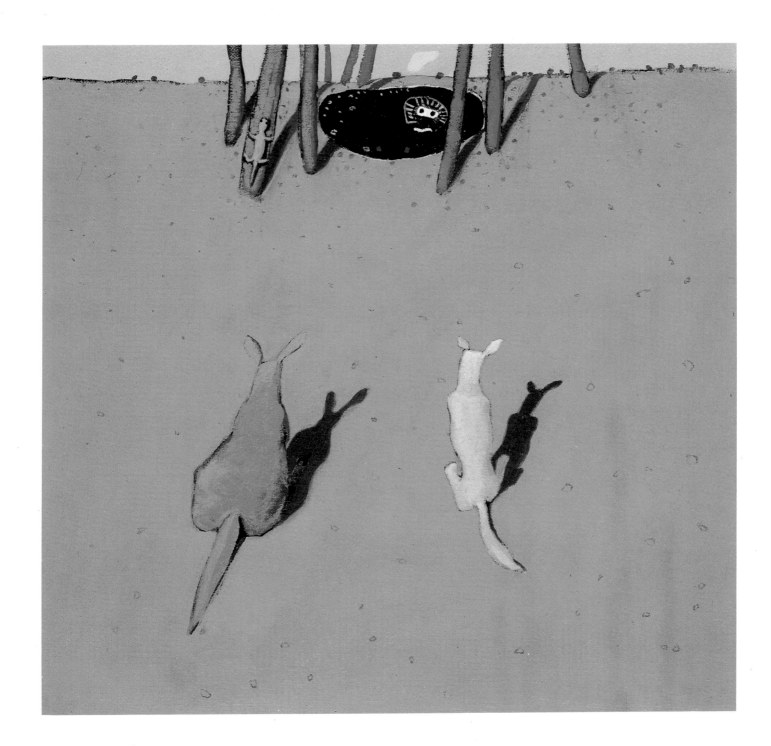

So they were left in the middle of Australia, Old Man Kangaroo and Yellow-Dog Dingo, and each said, "That's *your* fault."

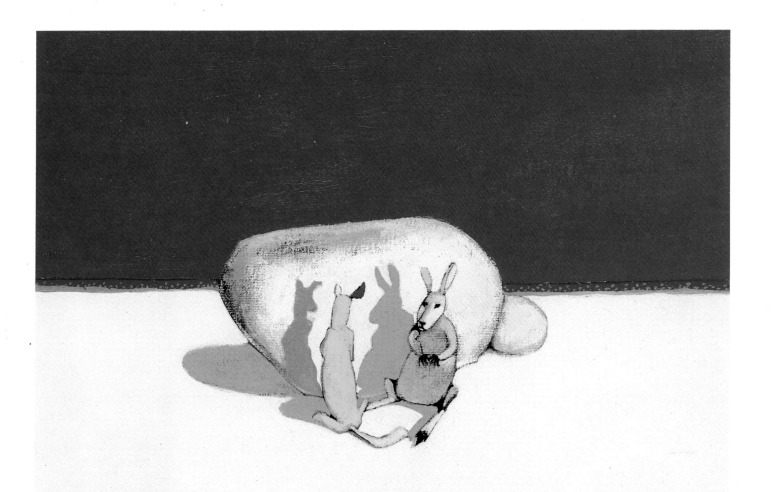

Songlines The Songlines emerge as invisible pathways connecting up all over Australia. Ancient tracks made of songs which tell of the creation of the land. The Aboriginals' religious duty is ritually to travel the land, singing the Ancestors' songs (the same songs as in Sing–Song), singing the world into being afresh.

These invisible pathways are known to Europeans as 'Dreaming Tracks' or 'Songlines', to the Aboriginals they are known as the 'Footprints of the Ancestors' or the 'Way of the Law'.

Aboriginal Creation myths tell of the legendary totemic beings who had wandered over the continent in the 'Dreamtime', singing out the name of everything that crossed their path–birds, animals, plants, rocks, waterholes – and so singing the world into existence.

In other words, the Sing–Song of Old Man Kangaroo would be a song that sang the kangaroo into existence.

Blue Gum Eucalypt tree. The Eucalypt tree grows in more than 500 different forms, the blue gum being just one form.

Mulga Scrub or bushes that grow in the desert lands of inland Australia.

Spinifex Grows in the hot, dry desert lands of inland Australia. One of the hardiest grasses in the world with needle–like leaves, and grows in circular clumps up to 6 metres in diameter.

Flinders Flinders ranges – red sandstone mountain range in South Australia, believed by the Aboriginals to be the work of the serpent Arkaroola who slithered among the drying waterholes in search of one final drink.

Tropics Tropics of Capricorn and Cancer – either of two imaginary circles about 23 1/2 degrees north and south of the equator above which the sun appears to turn at midsummer and midwinter.

Ti Trees Very common bush/tree found all over Australia. Bamboo like and grows up to 6 meters high.

Boomer Large kangaroo.